Tessa Moore

Dad *and the* Mad Cow Roundabout

Illustrated by Terry Myler

THE CHILDR

First published 2005 by
The Children's Press
45 Palmerston Road
Dublin 6

2 4 6 7 5 3 1

ISBN 1 901737 54 3

Typeset by Computertype Limited
Printed by Colour Books Limited

Contents

1 The Car

They all went out to see Dad's new car.

Dad, Mum, Loopy, Grandma and the twins, Rusty and Dusty.

It was a bright red car with an open top.

Dad stood proudly beside it.

'Brill!' said Rusty.

'Super!' said Dusty.

'If you ask me...' said Grandma.

'Nobody did,' muttered Dad.

'It's a lovely car,' said Mum.

'Call that a car!'

Grandma rolled her eyes and went back into the house.

'Where did you get it?' asked Loopy.

'It's a special car,' said Dad. 'Made for a film.'

'Gosh!' squealed the twins. 'What film?'

'Well, they meant to make one. Like James Bond. Then they ran out of money.'

It's a special car,

'How it is special?' asked Dusty. 'What does it do?'

'Well, I don't think it can *fly*,' said Dad. 'But it might have a few suprises under the bonnet. Watch this space!'

'Can we go for a drive now?' asked Rusty.

'Tomorrow,' promised Dad.

Uncle Joe appeared out of nowhere and walked around it.

'What did you pay for it?'

Dad told him.

Uncle Joe gave it a kick.

'Huh! They must have seen you coming.' And he walked off.

'Never mind, dear,' said Mum, 'It's a very nice car.'

Next morning, Dad said to
Mum, 'We'll drive down to Aunt
Millie's with that parcel you were
going to post. The twins can come
and Loopy will map-read.'

But when they got outside,
Grandma was in the front seat.

'She thinks she'll go for a bit
of fresh air,' said Mum. She
hurried back into the house.

'I have to be in the front seat,'
said Loopy. 'I have to map-read.'

'Map-read? Where are we off
to? Darkest Africa? Haven't you
heard of sign-posts?'

So Loopy got into the back with
the twins.

Uncle Joe came to see them off.
'Where are you headed?'

'We go south,' said Loopy, 'and
then west.'

'Beware,' said Uncle Joe in a
hollow put-on voice. 'Beware the
Mad Cow Roundabout!'

'We're not going anywhere near
the Mad Cow Roundabout,' said
Dad coldly.

'What's the Mad Cow Round-about?' asked Dusty.

'It's a traffic jam!'

'It's a traffic jam,' said Uncle Joe. 'Biggest in the world. Everything on wheels ends up there.'

'Why?' asked Rusty.

'Because if you're driving from Dublin, it's the main way onto the motorway. And if you're coming from the South or West, it's the main road into Dublin.'

13

'That's daft,' said Dusty.

'Daft? It's murder!'

'We are not,' repeated Dad,
'going near the Mad Cow, so
don't get all worked up about it.'

'Get a move on,' said Grandma,
'or we won't get anywhere. And
make sure I'm back in time for
my dinner. One o'clock sharp.
Bacon and cabbage.'

They came to a cross-roads.
'Which way?' asked Dad.
But the wording was half
hidden by the trees.

'One arm says "...th",' said
Loopy. 'The other says "...th". It
might be safer to go straight on.'
So they went straight on.

They came to another sign-post. 'It only says "North" and "South", ' said Loopy. 'No towns. And I don't know the road number. But Aunt Lucy is south.'

Suddenly the road did a U-turn. 'Now we're going north,' said Loopy. 'We must turn the car.'

'Can't,' said Rusty.

'One-way street,' said Dusty.

'If I'd known you didn't know where you were going,' said Grandma. 'I would have stayed at home.'

'Why didn't you?' snarled Dad.

'Don't worry, we'll soon be back on track,' said Loopy, trying to open up his map.

Then they heard the noise.

At first it had been a low hum.

Now it was getting louder.

And louder.

The road grew wider. Side roads snaked out of nowhere.

Cars and vans and trucks and

lorries a mile long stretched as far
as the eye could see.

Then a huge sign loomed up.

'It's the Mad Cow Roundabout,'
gasped Loopy.

'Joe *did* warn you!' croaked
Grandma. 'But would you listen?'

2 The Roundabout

'The main thing is to keep calm,' said Loopy.

'I am calm,' shouted Dad, jumping up and down. 'I just want to know which way to go.'

'I'll turn on my radio,' said Dusty. 'We'll get the traffic news.'

The traffic came to a full stop. 'At least now I can read the map,' said Loopy, spreading it out.

The nearby sign read: **Get in Lane Now**. The arrow for their lane pointed left.

'There are three lanes of traffic,' said Loopy. 'We should be in the middle lane. If we stay in this lane, we'll have to turn left.'

'That's back to Dublin,' said Dusty.

'But we've just come from Dublin,' said Loopy. 'We don't want take that lane.'

'Take it,' said Grandma, 'or
we'll be here all night.' She
glared at Dad. 'I can't see him
getting the hang of this set-up.'

'Maybe that's a good idea,' said
Loopy. 'We can always take a
back road to Aunt Millie's.'

Just then a beaten-up looking truck appeared on their left.

'Where does he think he's going?' said Dad.

'He's on a slip road,' said Loopy. 'He want to come into the roundabout.'

'Well, he can't. We're bumper to bumper. He'll just have to wait.'

They inched forward another few yards. The truck came up right beside them.

'My! My!' said the fatty who was driving. 'Did you ever see such a Mickey Mouse effort?'

'Oughtn't to be allowed on the road,' said the scruffy side-kick. 'No L-drivers. No kiddy cars.'

'If you're referring to my
car,' said Dad. 'It's a proper car.
Fully taxed and insured.'

'More than can be said for your
old jalopy,' added Loopy.

That made Fatty hopping mad.

'You mind your own *......
business,' roared Fatty. 'Do you
want a *...... punch in the nose?'

'Cover your ears!' said Loopy
to the twins. 'Don't listen!'

'You listen to me,' shouted
Fatty, stabbing his finger at
Dad. 'Push over and let me in.'

'Let him wait,' said Loopy.

'Move over, you half-wit,' said Fatty, as their lane began to move forward slowly. 'There's bags of room next door.'

So there was. The middle lane had driven on. So the red car was crowded into the middle lane.

'I hope we can get back into
the outside lane,' said Loopy.
'There seems to be a big tailback.'
The middle lane stopped again.

At the exit to the roundabout,
the truck caught up with them.
'What do you know, Joe!'
sneered Fatty. 'The Red Peril has
crawled a few yards, so it has.'

'There's a draught,' said Grandma. 'It's hitting my bad arm.'

'How could there be a draught?' asked Loopy. 'The windows are down.'

'Tell her it's known as fresh air in our part of the country,' said Dad.

'Grandma, what's written under the buttons? There should be one to put up the windows. Check.'

'I can't read anything,' said Grandma. 'I haven't got my reading glasses with me.'

She pressed a button. There was a faint grinding noise.

'What was that?' asked Rusty.

No one had heard anything.

At that moment there was a roar from the truck.

'We have a flat!' shouted Fatty.

As the traffic was still stopped, the side-kick got out.

'Something slashed our front tyre,' he snivelled. 'It's flat as a pancake!'

'If you did it, I'll murder you,'
said Fatty to Dad.

'Don't be stupid,' said Loopy.
'How could we do it? This isn't a
James Bond movie. There isn't a
knife under the car.'

'There is though,' whispered Dusty. 'It just slid out. She pressed a button marked "Tyre Slasher".'

'Must be one of the "surprises",' said Rusty. 'Don't mention it.'

I saw it...

'Drive on,' said Grandma. 'Do you want to be murdered?'

So they shot off.

As they rejoined the traffic jam, a voice came over the radio.

'Your traffic update. A truck has broken down at the Dublin exit to the Mad Cow Roundabout. That lane is partly blocked and there's a big tailback. Expect long delays.'

'Brill!' said Loopy. 'Now we can get back into the outside lane.'

3 Trouble

'We've been stuck here for over an hour!' said Grandma.

'Don't blame me,' said Dad. 'It's called gridlock.'

'Relax,' said Loopy. 'A Merc or a SVU won't get past that truck. Then we move into the left lane.'

The chance came even sooner.
'Quick!' said Rusty. 'The man
next door is reading his paper.'
But when traffic moved on
again, Dad still dithered.

Grandma grabbed the wheel
and gave it a twist.
The car veered left.

The red car shot into the left lane. Just then the BMW in the left lane sprang into action.

It caught Dad's car on the tail. 'You hit me!' screamed the driver. He looked like a gorilla.

'No, you hit us,' said Loopy.

At the next traffic stop, they both got out.

'There's a new scratch on my fender,' said the gorilla.

'There are that many dints on it already,' said Loopy, 'that you wouldn't notice another.'

Next moment, the gorilla ran round the car and grabbed Dad by the neck, knocking his glasses off.

'I'm going to sue you. Gimme the name of your insurance lot.'

'I will not,' said Dad.

'Then I'll knock your block off.'

'Be careful, dear,' said the BMW. 'Think of your heart.'

'It's going to rain,' said Grandma. 'I want to put the roof up.'

'Come on out, you coward,' roared the gorilla to Dad.

'Try another button,' said Dusty to Grandma.

So she pressed two more.

Next moment the car roofed over and the windows slid up.

The gorilla's arm was caught between the roof and the window.

'Help!' he screamed. 'My arm is coming off!'

'The windows. Put them down,' shouted Loopy to Grandma.

But it was five minutes before she found the right button.

When the window went down,
the gorilla fell back into the road.
A small crowd gathered round.

'I think we should make a quick
getaway,' said Loopy, ' while the
coast is clear.'

As the red car streaked off,
there was the sound of a siren.

4 More Trouble

They soon had to stop again.

'At this rate,' said Grandma, 'we won't be home till Christmas.'

'It's not our fault,' said Loopy. 'Everyone gets stuck in the Mad Cow Roundabout.'

'And who got us into it?'

But just as they came up to the exit turn-off, a new lane appeared, thick with traffic.

'That's not fair!' protested Loopy. 'We're blocked in again.'

Suddenly the traffic began to move again. Quickly.

The exit shot past.

'It's not our fault,' said Loopy. 'There's just too much traffic.

'Why is there so much traffic?'
asked Dusty.

'Mostly people trying to get to
work,' said Dad. 'They work in
the towns and they live in the
next county, hours away.'

'Why don't they live in the
towns?'

'They can't afford to buy a house there.'

'Cool!' said Dusty. 'Who thought that one up?'

'It's called Planning,' said Dad. 'Mostly done by people who don't use buses and trains. You won't find them queueing in the wind and the rain.'

'Some people,' said Grandma, 'know everything. Except how to fight their way out of a paper bag.'

The radio crackled:

'Facts of Life: Two out of three people travel to work by car.'

'Why don't people go by train?'

'There aren't enough trains. Even if there were, there aren't enough tracks for them to run on.'

'Why don't they build more?'

'They don't seem to have any plans for more trains. Most of the money spent goes on roads – eight out of every ten euro.'

'Then why don't people use buses?'

'They aren't enough of those either. Or drivers. So most people have to use their cars.'

One person one car!

The radio crackled again:

'Three out of every cars on the road has only one person in it.'

'Why...?' began Rusty.

'You two just ask questions,' cut in Loopy. 'Try and help us to get out of this mess.'

'But what can we do?'

'Keep an eye out for the sign-posts. We're missing all the traffic signs.'

'But we can't see anything.'

Nor could anyone.

A huge convoy of lorries had drawn up on their left. Another blocked the right-hand lane.

'This is daft,' said Dad. 'I'm sure I read that all the big lorries had to go through the new tunnel.'

'That was the idea.'

'Then why don't they?'

'The tunnel isn't high enough. They won't fit.'

The traffic began to move again. The huge convoy on the left took the left Exit road.

And, as if on cue, a whole new lane appeared.

An empty lane!

'Get into it,' screamed Loopy, 'before anyone else does!'

So the red car bobbed happily into the empty left-hand lane.

'Why are there no cars?' asked Rusty.

'It must be after rush hour.'

'This is more like it,' said Dad.
'We'll soon be at Aunt Millie's.'

All of a sudden, there was a
high-pitched sound. And a kind of
clanking.

'There's something behind us,'
said Rusty.

'It's a tram!' gasped Dusty.

'We're on the Luas line,' said
Loopy.

They looked back.

The driver was leaning out of the cab, screaming at them.

'Didn't you see the lights?'

'Of course I didn't,' snapped Dad. 'I can't see through vans.'

'It's raining again,' said Grandma. 'Where's that button?'

She pressed a button and a dense cloud of smoke arose from the back of the red car.

There was a squeal of brakes, screams, a dull dragging sound.

'She pressed a button marked SMOKE,' said Dusty to Rusty.

When they looked back, the Luas was gone.

Just then a sign loomed up. EXIT!

'Don't miss it!' shouted Loopy. The car shot out left.

'We're out!' said Loopy. 'We're out of the Mad Cow Roundabout!'

'Home!' croaked Dad.

'I want a Rest Stop now,' said Grandma. So they stopped at the first café they saw.

Grandma went to the 'Ladies'.

Dad drank cup after cup of black coffee. His eyes were wild and his hands were shaking. He didn't say a thing when the twins ate doughnut after doughnut.

A police car stopped before the café and four garda rushed in.

'What on earth are you up to?' they shouted. 'You've caused a major holdup. Nearly killed a man. And derailed the Luas.'

'It wasn't our fault...' Dad began to explain.

'Hold on a mo,' said one of the garda, taking out a new notebook and sharpening his pencil. 'This is going to take some time...'

It was almost dark when the red car limped home.

'Good timing,' said Loopy. 'I don't think Dad knew where the lights were.'

Uncle Joe was in the kitchen.

'Pity you missed dinner. Lovely bit of bacon.'

'I'll make some sandwiches,' said Mum, hurrying off. 'I'll see if there's anything left in the fridge.'

Two days later the postman
called.

'You left this behind in the
Ritz Café,' he said, 'and they've
sent it back to you.'

It was Aunt Millie's parcel.

'Can we take it down again?'
asked the twins. 'Tomorrow?'

'Over my dead body,' said
Grandma.

'That,' muttered Dad, 'could be
arranged.'

Mum wrote Aunt Millie's address on the parcel and handed it back to the postman. 'I think' she said, 'it might be quicker by post.'

'What a pity,' said Rusty. 'We could have tried out more buttons.'

'Grown-ups,' said Dusty, 'have just no sense of adventure.'

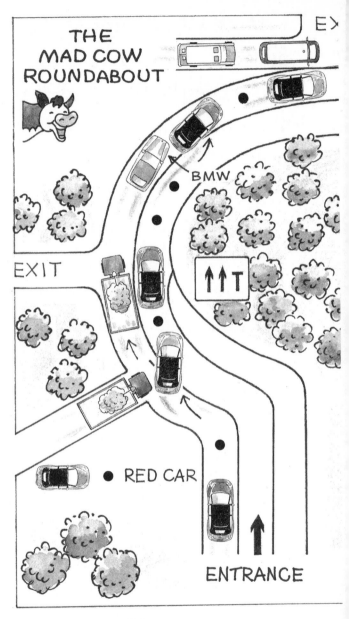

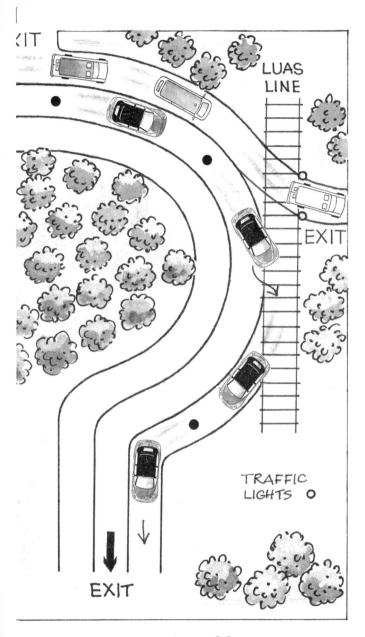

Chimps – very easy books for beginners
Large type
Short words
Short sentences
An illustration on every page
And fun!
With a twist in the tale!

This is the seventh **Chimp** *– the other six are:*
Cookie the Cat
Cookie and Curley
Flash Fox and Bono Bear
Two Mad Dogs
Back Up the Beanstalk
Where's Jacko?

Tessa Moore *comes from Waterford,
now lives in Dublin.*
Terry Myler, *who lives in Wicklow,
has illustrated all the* **Chimps.**